'A beautifully presented book...the boy's clear, lively voice literally jumps off the page.' READING TIME, 1998

'A warm and engaging tale which celebrates the importance of family and culture.' JOURNEY, 1998

'A narrative told from somewhere between childhood and adolescence, from some place between black and white Australia. The tale itself is sometimes painful, sometimes playful, but always enjoyable.' MAGPIES, 1998

'Charming and insightful, *My Girragundji* cleverly weaves childhood magic with issues of racism, adolescence and courage. Children will love this cross-cultural tale. Read it to them if necessary.' AUSSIE POST, 1998

'A deceptively slender book...it has an unexpected range and depth.' THE ADELAIDE ADVERTISER, 1999

'When Pryor visited his mother's homeland, Yarrabah, his Uncle Henry Fourmile gave him the Kunggandji word for green tree frog – girragundji, to use in the title.' KOORI MAIL, 1999

'This fascinating story gives a rare insight into growing up between two worlds, and rites of passage in Aboriginal culture.' UK BEST BOOK GUIDE, 2003

Also by
Meme McDonald
and **Boori Monty Pryor**

The Binna Binna Man
Njunjul the Sun
Maybe Tomorrow
Flytrap

ALSO BY **MEME McDONALD**

Love like Water

ALSO BY **BOORI MONTY PRYOR**

Shake a Leg
illustrated by Jan Ormerod

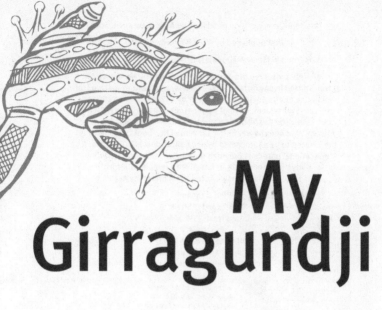

My Girragundji

20th anniversary edition

MEME McDONALD
& BOORI MONTY PRYOR

Photographs by Meme McDonald

ALLEN&UNWIN
SYDNEY • MELBOURNE • AUCKLAND • LONDON

This anniversary edition published by Allen & Unwin in 2018

First published by Allen & Unwin in 1998

Allen & Unwin
83 Alexander Street
Crows Nest NSW 2065
Australia
Phone: (61 2) 8425 0100
Email: info@allenandunwin.com
Web: www.allenandunwin.com

A catalogue record for this
book is available from the
National Library of Australia

ISBN 978 1 76029 710 7

For teaching resources, explore
www.allenandunwin.com/resources/for-teachers

Cover and text photographs by Meme McDonald
Frog illustration by Shane Nagle and Lillian Fourmile
Frog and snake courtesy of the Royal Melbourne Zoo
Design and typesetting by Ruth Grüner

Printed in Australia by McPherson's Printing Group

1 3 5 7 9 10 8 6 4 2

Meme McDonald gratefully acknowledges the support
of the Australia Council Community Cultural Development Fund
in granting her a Fellowship.

Australian Government

Australia
Council
for the Arts

for Girragundji Joe

and the seven Pryor sisters:

Sue, Cilla, Chrissy, Kimmy, Chubby, Chicky, Toni

with thanks to Grace Cockatoo

M.M. & B.M.P.

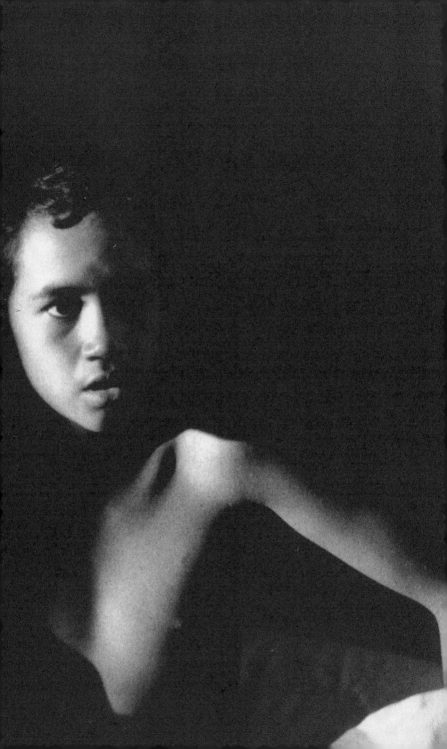

There's a bad spirit in
our house. The Hairyman.
Aunty Lil's got a good hairyman
in her house. He plays tricks on her
like pinching her cup of tea and
that, but it's all in fun. The Hairyman
in our house is bad, real bad.
He's as ugly as ugly gets and he
stinks. You touch this kind of
hairyman and you lose your voice
or choke to death or just die.
That can happen. You do the wrong
thing by these spirits and you
can just drop dead. My cousins'
uncle's brother did.

The Hairyman grabbed one of my sisters, you know. I've got seven of them. How unlucky is that? Seven sisters! He could have grabbed half a dozen of them for all I care. They sleep in the next room.

'You can't come in here. It's the girls' room!'

So what? We've got our own room. My brother Nicky sleeps across that side, and Paul and Rocco sleep head to toe in the bed on the wall.

One end of my bed is next to the louvre

 windows. I never sleep with my head up there. Too scared a hand will come through and grab me in my sleep.

I'm the oldest of us boys. The rest of them wouldn't be any good if the Hairyman had me. They'd be jammin' up, falling over each other trying to get out the door.

Anyway, one night the Hairyman –
that's what us mob call those spirits –
he grabbed my big sister by the throat.
We were all chasing through the house.
My big sister, Sue, thought she was gonna
scare the rest of us, so she hid in the

 darkest room and
kept real quiet.
None of us could
find her. Then all of
a sudden we heard
her screaming
her lungs out.
We raced in to
see what had
happened.
She was still
screaming,
with her hands
rubbing at her neck. Nearly turned white
she had, white as a migaloo, a whitefulla.

11

She was crying and cursing and saying it must have been one of us boys muckin' around. But she knew it wasn't any of us. She felt those hands around her neck and they were hairy, wrinkly, yucky, old hands, like Quinkin hands – that's what the old people call those spirits.

With her screaming and us running, that Hairyman took off, but we knew he'd be back.

I'm way too old to wet the bed, but there's no way I'm getting up to go to the gulmra, the dunny. Not down the hall, through the kitchen and all the way out the back. Not with that Hairyman in the house. It's dark out there.

I can't call out to my dad neither. I tried that one night but the voice got stuck in my neck like a fish bone. So, I lie in bed

and hold my knees together tight for as long as I can. Sometimes I can't.

I'm real shame, too. This migaloo jalbu, Sharyn, smiled at me in maths today. One of those smiles that sticks to you like ripe mango. I tried to smile back. The best I could do was a sort of little chonky-apple smile, 'cause I know the truth. I'm still a bed-wetter.

I can't go to sleep. The music's turned up and the arguments have started. There's something funny about the night that makes grown-ups go stupid and call each other names. Maybe it's their way of scaring off the Hairyman. Maybe it's just the grog in them.

My mum reckons our people are the strongest in the world, but that drink there takes your strength away, she says. I can see it in some of those fullas' eyes. Like they've sprung a leak and the sea's come rushing in to fill them up. They're drowning inside with all that drink. When they start yelling, it's like they're calling out from the bottom of the dark sea.

I'm trying to make that sleep wash over me, carry me away in its arms. I'm trying not to think about the Hairyman. I'm telling myself he won't be coming round while all the noise keeps up. Mozzies are nagging at me.

The night is that long I think the sun has given up on us. But it hasn't. The day has a quiet about it like it's been

called off. I stroll about when the rest
of them are still sleeping, checking for
dropped coins.

The rain poured down in the night. The
water'll be coming up under our house.
You've got to watch out for snakes this
time of year.

Chicky, my littlest sister, starts to tease.
'Sharyn's got the hots for you, na na
nanaa na!' She races back to the girls'
room.

I know the others have put her up to it,
I can hear their stupid giggling.

'Sharyn?!' I spit the name out like I've
just swallowed a blowfly. 'You lot are
sick.'

I go back to my room and dream about
kissing. They reckon you just touch lips
then poke your tongue out. Yuck! No
wonder you have to do it with your eyes
closed.

Another day comes up and I dawdle down our steamy street to school. I don't reckon you need to rush, but. It's not like school's gonna run away on you. I wish! I can feel a cloud of adults' anger following me like a bad smell. They should keep their yelling to themselves. It's not my fault their heads hurt. I don't reckon Sharyn will smile at me today.

My street is pretty good. I know all the kids. Further on, I still know all the kids, but sometimes they don't want to know me.

Eh, look out! She's there again. That migaloo jalbu, Sharyn. Hanging off her front fence. She's watching me go past. She's giving me that smile, that mango-mouth one. Maybe migaloos can't see those clouds that follow you on bad days.

I look across at her in class. I try to smile back. I go all fizzy inside, like I've eaten a bucketful of sherbet. Then the bell rings and all her mates come round squealing 'Shaz' this and 'Shazza' that. You'd reckon she'd never seen me before, or something. They rush out into the yard like a pile of scrap papers caught up in the wind. Doesn't matter, but, 'cause I know she's still smiling for me on the inside.

Anyway, I've got to keep my mind on what's happening. There's not always trouble. Not every day. But you've got to watch yourself. It can get rough out there. Words come yelling at you that hurt. And if you let your fists fly in anger you only hurt more. My dad taught me that. 'Never fight when you're angry. You'll always lose.'

I wait for that puffed-up, freckle-faced, migaloo bully boy, Stacey Straun, to start. He comes up behind me on the verandah and bangs me with his school bag. 'Yuck!'

he says. 'Now I'll have to get my mum to scrub it clean.'

I'm not angry, honest. I just want to bust him up real bad. I get ready to knuckle up, shaping up to the big, fat pig.

Dad says: 'Don't worry about being skinny, just stay on your toes.'

Now, I'm dancing all over the place like Michael Jackson.

Then I hear my dad again. 'Forget about being fancy. Forget about Michael effin' What's-his-face. Mohammed Ali, there's your man. Never take your eye off the enemy.'

Then I start praying, 'Please, God, whoever you are. I'm sorry I don't go to church, or say prayers every night neither, but could you please let me bust up Stacey Straun's fat face? Just this once? Bust him open like a rotten tomato? Pretty please?'

That night I go to bed with a busted lip and a thumping head. The busted lip I can wear, but when your mum clips you over the ear for getting into fights, and your dad gets stuck into you for losing, that hurts. How can you win?

I bury my head in the pillow to block out the noise. Mozzies are buzzing abuse again. You scratch a mozzie bite and it fights back till you've got a big sore. Same with the adults arguing. When everyone comes round at night for a charge up, a drink, any little thing ends in a punch-up. But that's not the end of it. Then there's the howlin' and the huggin' to make up for it, till the next night. I'm wondering what's the point of living.

The heat is wrapping round me
tight. I roll over and wait. I'm trying not
to listen for the Hairyman. He won't
come yet. Not till the racket dies down
out the back. Not till it's real quiet.

There it is.
Shhhkkk . . .
creak . . .
Shhhhkkk .
creak . . .

I know where he is by

the sound of his feet on

the lino. They stop in the

doorway of our room.

I watch the handle move.

Honest, truth and hope to

die, the handle is moving.

The door is opening.

I can't breathe. The heat

won't leave me alone.

It's hugging me real close.

I try and scream. I can't.

   Plop! Something lands

on me. **Help!** My voice

gets stuck. He's got me.

He's really got me this

time. I can feel his hands

around my throat. Let go!

I go to grab his hands.

Get off me!

   Hang on, they're my

hands. They're my hands

around my neck. You idiot,
let go of yourself! But
there's something wet on
my face. I can't move or it
might spread. It's pinning
me down. I'm gonna die.
Honest, I didn't really want
to die, I was only gammin',
only joking. Please help
me, my ancestors. I don't
want to die!

Plop! It hopped. Now
it's on my forehead. Plop,
again. It's on my cheek.
It's . . . it's . . . the green
slime. Oh no! A slow and
painful death. No . . .
it's . . . a . . . frog?

A frog! A little, green,
tree frog. A beautiful
little girragundji.

'Where did you come
from?' I'm breathing
again. I'm gonna
live. 'Where
you come
from,
little
fulla?'

Maybe them old people did hear me. Maybe the rain pouring down and the water coming up under our house scared this little one.

'Big snakes out there, yibulla. You gotta watch out for them big fulla snakes. They can gobble you right up. You stay in here with me, you little darlin'. We can look after each other.'

Her moist little feet stick to my skin. They tickle. Slowly, I reach out my hand to stroke her. She's so close. She peers into my eyes like she's looking down a telescope, right into my heart. Funniest thing is, I can see right through her eyes and into her heart, too. No one's ever looked at me like that. I feel safe.

I know those old people sent her to protect my spirit. They do that sort of thing. She came to me just when I needed her. She stays with me all through the dark nights. I don't have to worry about squishing her in the bed 'cause she knows which way I'm gonna roll even before I do.

My sisters know I've got her in my room. When Mum calls out for one of the older girls to wake us boys up, I wait for them. I hear them creeping up to the door, giggling. They've got a wet washer to chuck at me. So what? I leap up and run at them, something green in my hand. They scream back down the hallway, and still I'm chasing.

Chicky leaps straight out the window. She howls like a wild cat when she lands in the rose bush. I laugh.

Mum yells, 'What's the matter?'

I'm all innocent. 'Didn't do nothing,' I say. I open up my hands. 'I was only gammin'. Look, it's a leaf. Those girls are scaredy cats. I wouldn't chase them with my precious girragundji.'

I get a clip over the ear, but it's worth the pain just to hear my sisters squeal like that. They might be smarter at maths and pi-r-squared and playing cards, but I can still scare the living daylights out of them, even the big ones, even Sue and Cilla.

The bullies don't seem so big now my girragundji's with me. On school mornings, I don't have to fake a belly-ache no more. My mum hardly ever fell for

that one anyway, but. Getting busted up
at school doesn't hurt that much, now I
know she's there, my girragundji. Getting
busted up at home doesn't hurt that much
neither.

Before I head off to school, I make sure
she's right for the day. Louvres open so
she can hop across to the hibiscus tree,
and out and about. A little bowl of water
in case she wants a drink and a cool-
down. I get Mum to promise not to shift

anything. I tell my girragundji I'll be back as soon as I can with some treats.

I feed her moths. Not the really big ones, though, or she can't get them down. But big enough for a good feed.

I know she waits for me on the windowsill. I even think she might hear the sound of my feet on the front steps. Bare feet on bare wood, then padding down the hallway, alive like a frog. Not dead feet dragging like that other sound that gets you in the neck. *Shhhkkk . . . creak . . . shhhkkk . . . creak . . .* No, she knows my feet on the lino. I never have to call her. Don't know what I would call her anyway.

You can tell a lot from eyes. When I look in my gundji's eyes, she speaks to me. She has the sweetest voice. I stroke her, gently as a cool breeze, then sit her up on the window ledge. I can hear my cousins kicking the footy. She knows I'll be back.

My cousin Kevin is staying at our place.
He's real tough. He reckons only kids are
scared of Quinkins. I agree. All the other
scaredy cats are sleeping quieter, just
'cause their big cus is on the couch.

He's good at footy, too. He teaches
me a lot.
He reckons,
when you
play footy,

it doesn't matter if you're one of them or one of us, it's how high you can jump or how long you can kick.

I can kick a long way when I'm fired up. They reckon I'll play in the big league one day. I could. Plenty do. I'd play with boots on then. Deadly, eh? Then she'd smile at me, Sharyn, no matter who's about. No shame then. I smiled at her the other day. One of those big mango-mouth smiles. Even called her Shaz.

When I get angry, I think of my gundji. I watch how she pushes down with her legs and leaps so high. I take that anger and I push him down into my legs. I run with that anger. I run so hard I beat the lot of them. I kick further than anyone, even with no boots on. I climb higher into the air. No one can catch me now. Not even with their curses. And I laugh and call to my girragundji to take me higher.

Back home, I crash. Lungs burning. Legs like jelly. Starving. Mum's cutting back the hibiscus. I plead with her to leave a branch just a frog's jump from the louvres.

Why are mums so mean? I reckon they can read your mind even with your eyes closed, and still they suit themselves. They know you want something so bad you'll do the dishes for a week, still they hold out on you. But sometimes, just when you give up on them, they come good. 'All right, my boy,' she says, and I know I'm gonna love her for the rest of my life.

I've got a big mob of mozzies for Gundji in my lunch-box. Got them on the way home, down the creek.

Mum goes right off when we squash them on the walls, 'specially when they're full of blood. She reckons the girls never do it in their room, but I don't reckon that's true. They're sneaky, that lot. I've seen the muck on the washer where they've cleaned up before they get caught. Thump! Blood red splotches on the lime green.

I used to get a hiding for that, but my patch is always clean now. Gundji plucks them out of the air with her long tongue while I'm sleeping. Tzzztz! Just like that. She sits on my forehead. Tzzztz!

Little beads of water have collected in the pores of her soft, green skin. I stroke them away. I lay a trail of mozzies down on the windowsill in front of her. She waits. She never grabs. I lie back with my head next to her, at the louvre end, and lift my shirt up. I wait. Her throat beats with breath. My breath stands still. Her tongue darts out and lassoes three mozzies in one hit. Then, plop, down onto my chest. The first touch of her feet shocks my skin. But the kind of shock that makes you tingle and suck your breath in with the thrill. Our hearts beat together. She gobbles up the mozzies.

I never used to lie with my head up this end. Now my girragundji's with me, I sleep with my head up the louvre end all the time.

It's the middle of the night and I'm busting. Gundji's there. I get up. It's not so dark. I walk out into the night. She's on my shoulder. I'm walking down the hall, through the kitchen, out the back and into the gulmra, the dunny, all the way in the dark, with her right there.

What a relief.

She looks across at me. Right into my eyes. 'Aren't you finished yet?'

I give it a shake, then hold her in my hands as I take off back to bed. I lay there with my heart racing. I did it. He didn't get me. Thank you, Gundji. I stroke her to sleep.

Hell, what's that? Someone's screaming. All the hairs on my body stand up. I lie low. Someone's running at me. A huge big fulla yelling and thrashing the air. He's jumped into my bed.

'Eh, look out, you big sook! Watch out for Gundji, you idiot.'

It's cousin Kevin. 'Stuff your frog, the . . . Hairyman . . . he . . . was breathin' down m' neck!'

Even big Kev is scared. I know I'm stretching it now, but I tell him, 'Lay down here then. Gundji'll keep us safe.'

That was me speaking, speaking like a grown-up. Not cousin Kevin. It was *me*! My darling girragundji grabs a mozzie right on cue. 'Tzzztz!' I shock myself to sleep.

With her watching over me, I have beautiful dreams. I dream of being out in the boat down the Bohle with my dad. That's our special place where the river meets the sea. It's their place really, my Aunty Joyce and Uncle Arthur's place. But they reckon it's our place, and Dad doesn't argue with that 'cause he reckons that's right. They're white and we're black

and I don't know whose place the Bohle
is, it just is, and they'll always be our
aunty and uncle.

I dream I'm crocodile-sliding down the
soft, sandy bank and into the cool water.

I dream of curling up with a belly full
of mud crab and wirrell beside our camp
fire. I dream those dreams you never want
the dawn to chase away.

Dad's down packing the ute. The sun isn't even up yet. I love it when you get a head start on the day. We're going down the Bohle, to our special place where the river meets the sea. I hope the car starts.

I feel different today. Like a bird about to take its first flight. This trip, I know something important is gonna happen. I can't wait, but I'm all nervous.

All us kids pile in the back. Gundji watches from the window ledge. She knows it's a special day, too. She said it's like she's coming with me, even though she's not. She said our spirits are always together. That made me want to cry. She just kept saying it over and over, and said

I must never forget. 'Our spirits will always be together, no matter what.'

I know each bump of the road as we get close to Uncle Arthur and Aunty Joyce's. They've got a boat, and us kids take turns. When it's my turn to stay back, I play in the mangroves. Course you've got to watch out in there. You got to know where to go and where not to go. You got to listen when those old fullas tell you about the crocodile. It's no joke, neither. You don't listen, you die. Quick as that they get you.

When I know I'm in a safe place, I muck about in the mangroves like the day'll never end.

There's everything in there. You move, the whole place goes dead quiet. Not even a breath. You stop still, everything else moves. Things growing and crawling and burrowing and climbing, buzzing and squelching and farting. That mangrove smell is the sweetest. Like the breath of the most secret place on earth.

You can be yourself in a place you belong. I wonder if Shaz would like it in here. On second thoughts, I wouldn't risk bringing her down. Most migaloos have got funny ideas about mud and dirt. We been told you belong to that earth there. It's your mother. But they been treating him like some stranger or something. Always washing themselves and cleaning up. Maybe that's how they got to be white in the first place.

My dad turns to me. 'It's time you learnt to kill food to eat, my boy.'

So this is it. I wish my gundji was here. I try and remember that she really is. We walk down to the edge of the sea.

Dad gets me to grab the turtle. He shows me how to flip him on his back and take him by the throat. I call on my gundji, 'Make me strong. Make me know I have that strength inside of me.'

The knife is long and sharp and I feel my knees give way. I want to let him go. My dad is telling me which way to cut him, and I have to be strong. I am strong and I see the blood squirt and the turtle thrash around on his back, gasping for breath.

I hear my dad: 'Turtle gives his life for you. You thank him for that, my boy. He gives his life so you can eat him and be strong. You got to respect that. You kill your own meat then you know to respect life. All life. That's the way things are.'

My dad teaches me lots of things, and I listen. Never to kill unless for food. And then to be careful not to kill the woman crab or fish. Turn him over first. If he's a woman, we let him go. This woman fish I caught, big one too, I held him up and looked him in the eye and said, 'Lucky you not a man.'

Then I give that one a big kiss and she swims away to make more fish.

I'm **tired** and **strong** on the way home. The rain pours down and washes away the little fulla me. I can't wait to see my girragundji. I look out for her as Dad turns into the yard. She's probably inside. There'll be water coming up. Coming up under our house. The snakes won't worry me. My mum reckons: 'They're as scared of you as you are of them, so let them be.' I reckon that's true.

When we get home all the lights are on. There's a big mob of cousins and aunties and uncles come over, but they're not charging up. They're all sitting round the table having cups of tea, waiting for us.

There's a lot of talking and carrying on. Mum seen the Hairyman in our boys' room. My aunty seen him too. He's a migaloo one, she reckons.

A whitefulla hairyman, how's that?

Aunty Lil reckons some bad people had done bad things to our people in this place a long time ago. Mum reckons something needs to be done about the Hairyman. She reckons we got to smoke the house to get rid of him.

My dad reckons we gotta get that church fulla in to do his business, too, just in case this Hairyman only knows whitefulla language.

I help Dad build a fire out the back and we have a big feed of turtle.

Everyone reckons we'll have to get Popeye, that's my grandad, over to do the smoking. He knows all our language and the right way to do these things. He was taught by the old people.

Uncle Shorty tells us lots of stories. I can't wait till Popeye comes. The fire stings my eyes. I close them and lie back and let the talk and the singing of the old songs soak in.

I'm dog tired by the time I go to bed. The best kind of tired, but, when all your worries have lifted like smoke on the breeze. My dad has taught me things, my aunties and uncles are round telling stories, and my Popeye is coming over soon to deal with the Hairyman for good.

My little brothers don't want to sleep in here tonight. They reckon they want to play it safe and wait till Popeye comes to do the smoking.

I won't sleep anywhere else. I lay down and stretch out, head to the louvres, and wait to be with my gundji. She'll hop across when she's ready. I got to be patient. I check the louvres are open. They are. I lay back. I hate waiting, but the smell of the smoke from the fire is sweet in my nostrils. It carries me into a deep sleep.

I hear talking in my dreams. I can't tell whether it's her voice or the sweet smoke or the Hairyman that is wrapping round me so close. 'Don't be afraid. Just look at me.'

I wake with a start. The doorknob turns. It does. It's him. The Hairyman. I heard his feet dragging on the lino.

Shhhkkk...

creak...

Shhhhkkk...

creak...

I'm lying out flat on my back, head to the louvres. Where's Gundji?

'Don't be afraid.' That's her voice. 'Remember our spirits are always together.'

Her voice is filling me up. I'm struggling to breathe with the heat that's hugging me. I'm struggling to be strong. I can feel him over that side near the door.

I grab that fear and push him down into my legs. I feel my Gundji leap inside me. I jump up. I'm standing on top of my bed ready to strike. But I can't look at him.

'The Hairyman is no different from you.'

No way, how can that be? Give me a look at him. I wanna look that fulla in the face and tell him to get lost. Nothing can stop me now. I open my eyes.

I look at him. I can only see his back. He's already turned to go. I can see real clearly, like I'm looking through big round eyes, her eyes. He's backing off. The Hairyman is scared of me, I know he is. He's shrinking back into the shadows. A cloud of horrible things that happened a long time ago is trailing him. That's his

bad smell, that stink following him.
I watch him slide away.

I can feel her heart in mine. My breath
is even. That fear has let me go.

I take my time to lie back down, then
drift like I'm in the arms of the ocean back
into sleep. I sleep like a man this night.

I'm up early, ready for
the day. I don't even care
if my sisters see me stop at
Sharyn's. So what? She's sitting
out the front, all white and pink stripes.
I'm easy with my 'g'day'. Just like that.
Cool. She's got that smile on again. I've
got one on, too. She starts talking. I'm not
hurrying. She likes footy. Says she's going
down to the match. Funny that. Just where
I'm headed. I want her to watch me.
I know I'll play well.

She's got her own bike. Pretty deadly!
We walk two blocks together then I race
ahead, kicking the footy. I've got that fizzy
sherbet in my belly again. I don't care.
I reckon she has too.

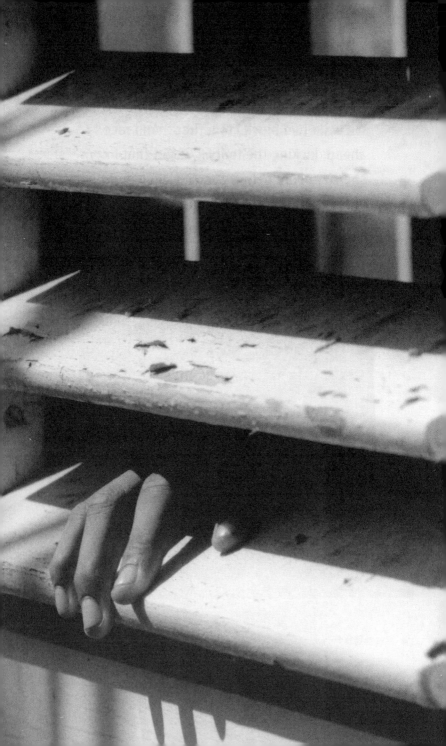

That night I spread out across the
bed. My dreams are full. I can hear the
rain coming down in bucket-loads on the
roof. I shut the louvres to stop my bed
getting soaked and go back to dreaming.

The storm stops. It's very quiet. I can
see me still out there flying down the
field, leaping for screamers; that strength
in my legs pushing down, kicking goals.
Shaz is watching. Yelling out for me. I'm a
hero, but I've only got eyes for her. All the
other jalbus will have to look elsewhere.
'Sorry, girls, I'm taken.' Eh, look out!
I laugh out loud. Sometimes I go real
stupid in my dreams.

It's nearly dawn. There's a sound
nudging me awake. I roll over, trying to
hold on to that dream. But that sound is
the worst. It rips through me like thunder.

I flick open the louvres.
It's her, calling out like
death from under the
house where the water
comes up. Fear grabs at
my heart and squeezes
tight. That water brings
the snakes. A snake has
got her, my girragundji,
I know it has.

I race down the hall,

grab the torch off the

fridge, out through the

kitchen, down the back

and round the side into

the dark. I don't care

about the Hairyman.

He can't touch me now.

I don't know whether

it's rain or tears, but

I can't see.

I'm gonna grab that snake by the throat and kill him forever. I try and squeeze under the house. I'm too big. I can't get through to her. There's nothing I can do. Girragundji, my girragundji, my darling girragundji.

I freeze in the dark. My mind leaves me and goes to her. I stroke her gently as a cool breeze. I whisper I love her. I can hear her. 'Our spirits . . . always . . . together . . . you are strong . . . no matter what.' Then she is gone. I lie in the mud crying like a rainstorm.

The next night takes a long time to come round. My heart hurts. Little Chicky gives me a hug when she finds out. I tell her I'm sorry I was a bully and I won't be needing to do that no more.

We sit on the front steps together and wait for Popeye. It's the weekend, and he should be coming to do the smoking today or tomorrow.

I never had
warts before,
I swear. Never ever.
I heard Sharyn's mum say you
can get them from touching too
many frogs. She's a migaloo, but,
and sometimes they don't know that
much about the way things are. Not Uncle
Arthur and Aunty Joyce of course. They're
migaloos but they understand lots of
things. Sharyn said her mum used to
throw salt on frogs to dry them up so they
wouldn't come in the house. I hope her
mum is right about the warts.

That month I grew warts on my fingers.
Sharyn said my warts are revolting and
I should go to the doctor. I kissed them
in front of her and said I didn't care. She
dropped me the next day. I was already
thinking she wasn't my type, but.

I found myself smiling at that Jody

Butler today. She smiled back. I heard her
talking about going bush with her family.
Reckons she loves it.

When the rain pours down and the
water comes up, I listen for the chorus
of croaks.
In the very centre of
that sound,
I hear my
girragundji.
She's still
there.
Always will
be. Protecting
me.

She's in my heart when I leap for a screamer, and then when I'm telling bullies to back off. She's there when I'm mucking about in the mangroves, and round the fire at night listening to the stories. She's there when I start smiling at girls, and even when I get a flogging from my dad.

She's there. That's the kind of thing that will never change.

How **My Girragundji** was written

My daughter Grace first prompted Boori
to tell the story of his pet frog. Boori's
childhood stories of his frog and the snake,
the hairyman and having seven sisters, the
mangroves, footy, and growing up between
two worlds, tickled my imagination too.
I began writing these stories down and
weaving them together. When Boori visited
his mother's homeland, Yarrabah, his Uncle
Henry Fourmile gave him the Kunggandji
word for green tree frog – girragundji. So we
called the story *My Girragundji*.

For over a year or so, Boori and I worked
together on *My Girragundji*. Then we took
a draft to Boori's family for them to read.
Laughter and jokes and yarns enriched the
story. A group of Boori's nephews and nieces

quickly overcame their shyness of the camera and were happy to take us down the beach to go fishing with their grandad, Monty. They led us into their favourite mangroves, kicking the footy along paths that Boori remembered well.

The story had come home to its beginning. Without the Pryor family this story would not be here for the telling. It is with their approval that we offer it to you and hope that it brings to life how different and how much the same growing up can be.

From **Meme**

The story of *My Girragundji* is still as alive
as it was when Grace first prompted Boori
to share it over twenty years ago. A story
of a courageous boy growing up between
two worlds seems only more necessary
as the years have passed. So too do the
laughter and jokes and yarns brought about
by a good story.

Since *My Girragundji* was first published
in 1998, the book has won several awards
and been chosen by Reading Australia as
one of twenty books of national significance
as part of their online program for schools.

My Girragundji has been adapted into
a stage play, and the third season toured
in July and August 2013. Canute Productions
in association with Glen Leitch Management
began the tour in Brisbane. The tour then

continued on to Newcastle, Sydney, and Canberra.

To our delight and eager anticipation, a feature film of *My Girragundji* is currently in script development, produced by Maggie Miles, Savage Films.

From its very beginning, *My Girragundji* empowered those it touched to overcome their fears, big or small. The story of a little tree frog, her gift was to stay with us through dark nights, to make us know we have strength inside us, no matter what.

We hope that you find the frog in your life, and leap from strength to strength.

MEME MCDONALD AND GRACE LOVELL,

NOVEMBER 2017

From **Boori**

Girragundji came alive through the inquiring mind of Meme's daughter, Grace. Grace's seven-year-old enthusiasm became infectious as she induced storytelling flashbacks. These flashbacks allowed me into my seven-year-old room of memories. Within this room were stories about my frog, seven sisters, three brothers and my mother and father. Individually, each of them started to breathe and come alive. Then, by the end of six weeks, they were all breathing together and telling their stories to everyone who would listen.

Growing and shaping a story takes the time it takes to become something lasting. Grace somehow knew that. Every night, there she was, chores done, teeth brushed, sitting tucked up in bed with her imaginary girragundji beside her. Unbeknown to us each night became an episode, and through Gracie's heart came the voice of girragundji to tell its story. This then became a gift, was placed in a box by Gracie, then given to all of us to share. Meme's gift was to open this precious box without damaging the frog. Meme did this by using great word craft and phrasing to honour its spirit. This then allowed the frog to leap into the dark scary places of one's mind, to bring hope if needed.

And now, as an award-winning book and soon-to-be major film, *My Girragundji* has leapt into the minds and hearts of adults and children alike, all over Australia and across the world, to bring hope in darkness and love for light to help make a brighter self.

Thank you, Gracie, and thank you, Meme, for your gifts, and for this slimy, green-caped crusader, *My Girragundji*.

BOORI MONTY PRYOR, JANUARY 2018

About the **authors**

MEME McDONALD'S family is from Western Queensland. Meme wrote books for children and adults. She also worked as a theatre director, specialising in dramatic outdoor performance events. Meme's first book, *Put Your Whole Self In*, won the 1993 Braille and Talking Book Award. The animation of her second book, *The Way of the Birds*, was nominated for an AFI Award and won a best-film award and the Cinanima Festival in Portugal. Meme McDonald's previous books – five of which were written in collaboration with Boori Monty Pryor – have won six major literary awards. Meme passed peacefully with the rising sun in December 2017.

BOORI MONTY PRYOR'S family is from North Queensland. His mother's people are Kunggandji and his father is from the Birra-gubba Nation. Boori is a performer, storyteller and didjeridoo player, who has worked in film, television, modelling, sport, music and theatre. In 1993 he received an award for the Promotion of Indigenous Culture from the National Aboriginal Islander Observance Committee. Boori was Australia's Children's Laureate in 2012 and 2013.

The first book Meme McDonald and Boori Monty Pryor wrote together was *Maybe Tomorrow*, which was shortlisted for the 1999 Children's Book Council of Australia awards. *My Girragundji* (Winner of the 1999 CBCA Award for Younger Readers) was followed by *The Binna Binna Man* (Winner of the Ether Turner Prize for Young

People's Literature, the Ethnic Affairs
Commission Award, and Book of the Year in
the 2000 NSW Premier's Literary Awards).
Boori's narration of *My Girragundji* and *The
Binna Binna Man* won the Australian Audio
Book of the Year Award. *Njunjul the Sun*,
the third book about the boy who features
in *My Girragundji* and *The Binna Binna
Man*, was published in 2002. *Flytrap* was
published in the same year.

Acknowledgements

Many thanks to Joe and Grace for inspiring *My Girragundji* to be written. Thanks also to the Pryor family for sharing so many memories, and to nieces and nephews: John Gool-in bulla (Crocodile) Baira, Frank Good-i-bun (Kangaroo) Baira, Isiah Dhyb-aroo (Possum) Blackman, Paulani Winitana, Shandell Prior, Sean Pryor, Nicky Bidju (Sea Hawk) Pryor and Caroline Gregory for the patience and beauty they gave to the photographs. Nicky Bidju features as the main character.

Thank you to Rosalind Price, Sue Flockhart, Ruth Grüner and Allen & Unwin for taking care with this story; to Linda Waters for giving her honest opinion and her encouragement; to Naomi Herzog, Robert Colvin and Brian Sollors for help and advice with photographs; to Lillian Fourmile, Allirah Tan, Greg Keating, Toni Pryor, Lawrence Massa, Renata Prior, Lance Riley, Father Mick Peters, Jenny Darling and Jacinta di Mase (Australian Literary Management), Glen Leitch (Young Australia Workshop), and to Ciaran Amar Chandran Ward for always being there.

the binna
binna man

Meme McDonald
& Boori Monty Pryor

Meme
McDonald
& Boori
Monty Pryor

Njunjul
the Sun

ANNIVERSARY · EDITION

MAYBE TOMORROW

'I can see right there in front of me
the face of a nation changing.'

BOORI MONTY PRYOR · MEME MCDONALD

Meme McDonald
& Boori Monty Pryor

flytrap